THE
OLD HALL DOBBY
A genuine ghost story

ORIGINALLY PUBLISHED BY D. ATKINSON,
KING STREET, ULVERSTON 1869

This version published in 2025

by Russell Holden

Page layout and cover design
© copyright Pixel Tweaks

ISBN: 978-1-9191665-4-4

Book production by Russell Holden
www.pixeltweakspublications.com

The following narrative, it is almost needless to state, is founded entirely on fact. Several persons now living can vouch for the correctness of the particulars which are still fresh in their memory. It has been reproduced from the Ulverston Mirror, with alterations and additions in its present handy form for the convenience of the general reader.

CONTENTS

CHAPTER I

"Now there spreaden a rumour that everich night
The rooms ihaunted been by many a sprite,
The miller avoucheth, and all thereabout
That they full oft hearen the hellish rout :
Some saine they hear the gingling of chains,
And some ho.th heard the psautries straines,
At midnight some the heeadless horse imeet,
And some espien a corse in a white sheet,
And oother things, faye, elfin, and elfe,
And shapes that fear createn to itself."

Gay's Imitation of Chaucer.

A REALLY good ghost story, if it possess the slightest claim to what is called by sensational writers " a tale of thrilling interest," is generally acceptable to the wonder-loving portion of the public, and all who delight in the mysterious, whether natural or supernatural.

"A ghost," according to Grose, is supposed to be the spirit of a person deceased, who is either commissioned to return for some especial errand, such as the discovery of a murder, to procure restitution of lands or money unjustly withheld from an orphan or widow, or, having committed some injustice while living, cannot rest till that is redressed. Sometimes the occasion of spirits revisiting this world is to inform their heir in what secret place, or private drawer in an old trunk, they had hidden the title deeds of the estate ; or where in troublesome times they buried their money or plate. Some ghosts of murdered persons, whose bodies have been secretly buried, cannot be at ease till their bones are taken up and deposited in consecrated ground, with all the rites of Christian burial."

Bearing in mind these remarks, as the opinion of a good authority in such matters, it will be easier to appreciate the following particulars respecting a dobby of widespread local fame, which haunted the Old Hall, a farmhouse situated about half a mile north-west of the town of Ulverston.

The Old Hall is a lone homestead, standing a little off the high road to Netherhouses, in the middle of a narrow valley, formed on the one side by the precipitous face of the Flan Hill, and the other by a corresponding elevation covered with trees, known as the Old Hall Wood. A footpath runs by the house and through the wood, making a favourite walk for the neighbouring townsfolk.

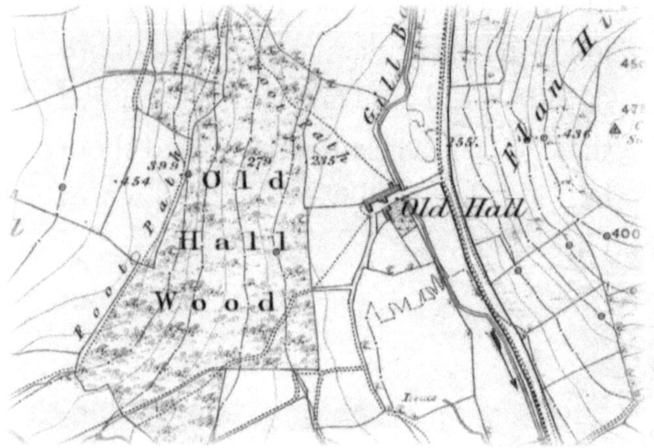

The aspect of the place at night is gloomy enough, and one might well imagine that a melancholic individual who had the ill-luck to pass by at " the very witching time of night, when graveyards yawn," would believe that

"In such a place as this, at such an hour,
If ancestry can be in aught believ'd,
Descending spirits have convers'd with man,
And told the secrets of the world unknown."

The farm originally formed part of the estate belonging to Conishead Priory, and tradition stated that a lady once visited the neighbourhood and put forward a claim to the property of which she declared she had been wrongfully deprived.

It was said she was a representative of the Dodding family, and came from some distant locality in Scotland.

It was further related that the mystery attached to the claimant and her extraordinary history was never cleared up, but that she disappeared in a very sudden and strange manner, and it was strongly suspected she was cruelly and foully murdered by hired assassins who thrust the body into an old well, which at one time existed near the point where the stream issuing from the rock in the Priory Park crosses the road, the old lodges on each side, with the gate, formerly standing there, having since been removed.

The spirit of this unhappy lady was believed by many to hover around the Old Hall, as if to assert her right to the estate, and to testify by its appearance the dreadful crime which had ended its natural course in the body so abruptly.

About fifty years ago there resided at the farm a worthy old couple named Rigg, of undoubted respectability, and in comfortable circumstances.

Mrs. Rigg had a nephew living at Bouth, who occasionally visited them at the Hall, and who was a decent, honest fellow, straight-forward, truthful, and reliable, having given them no reason to doubt his word on any previous occasion.

One night, after Ulverston market, when all the family were in bed, for it was nearly midnight, and the rain pouring in torrents, the old couple were aroused by loud knocking outside, and on getting up to ascertain the cause of the alarm they were astonished to find their nephew below, begging for a lodging.

He had lingered behind when market was over, and had been enjoying himself with some companions, taking his ease in his inn," the time flitting away so merrily that he scarcely noticed the lateness of the hour till warned, when he suddenly bethought himself of his old aunt, whose comfortable quarters seemed to possess greater charms for him than a ride to Bouth in face of such a storm of wind and rain as had by this time arisen. He was not drunk, but had just "a wee drap in his ee,"[1] and was (according to the testimony of his aunt, who was by no means disposed to be lenient with such transgressors) "sensible enough to understand what he was about."

---

1 "A wee drap in his ee" means "a small amount of alcohol in his eye", or more colloquially, "a small drink of alcohol".

A bed was accordingly provided for this unseasonable visitor, and after a little while the disturbed household once more resumed its usual quietude, the inmates being speedily wrapt in peaceful slumber.

CHAPTER II

This state of things was not fated to be of long duration, for the uncle and Aunt were, after the lapse of an hour or so, awakened by an energetic rapping at their bedroom door, which caused them no little concern.

It proved to be the nephew not long before admitted and safely stowed away in bed, who, with considerable anxiety, and ill-concealed alarm, declared most positively that he had been startled out of his sleep by a strange, unearthly noise, and on opening his eyes observed a strong light streaming in at the window.

He jumped out of bed and rushed to the casement expecting to see something on fire about the premises, but instead of that there appeared in the orchard an apparition of a most unusual character, so distinctly visible that he was able without the least difficulty to make out every particular of dress and manner.

He described the figure as that of a lady, walking with stately and dignified mien, and yet wearing an expression of sadness upon her countenance that would have melted the heart of any one, even though it were of adamantine hardness. He hurriedly ran over the articles of her dress, their style and arrangement, especially noticing the quaint dress skirt, flounced as high as the knees, and the odd looking bonnet, with its large crown and short high peaked front.

The old people yielded to his urgent request, and accompanied him to his room with all haste, but they were too late, the spectre had vanished, and they were left to ponder over this very mysterious occurrence.

Next morning, and ever after, the young man persisted in his story, maintaining with positive earnestness the truth of his assertions, and when questioned upon the subject of his nocturnal adventure, detailed with minute exactness the position, attitude, clothing, and features of his midnight visitor. He stoutly declared it was no "dream of waking fancy," but "a real, genuine dobby, and no mistake."

The news of this affair spread far and wide, and soon reached the ears of Colonel Braddyll, of Conishead Priory, the owner of the farm, who sent for Mrs. Rigg, and interrogated her closely on the circumstance.

Taking the old lady on the conclusion of her strange narrative, to another part of the Priory, he led her to several old family portraits hanging in the order of their succession, and directed her attention to one in particular, which bore an unmistakable similitude to the apparition her nephew had described, and they were both astounded at the marvellous accuracy with which it had unconsciously been pourtrayed.

As might be expected, this wonderful coincidence added greatly to the fame of the story, and the Old Hall became invested with a degree of interest and importance it had never before possessed.

In answer to Colonel Braddyll's inquiries, Mrs. Rigg said they had often heard queer kinds of noises about the house, particularly in the kitchen, after they had retired to bed, and in the room above, with rattling and scuffling, as if persons were moving about, but they had attributed these sounds to the rats, which abounded in the walls and floors of the old house.

Soon after this event the old farmer and his wife retired to Channel House, in Pennington, and the Old Hall was next occupied by one I____M____ who resided there for many years. In the meantime, the "Old Hall Dobby" had become a "recognised institution," and the house enjoyed the unenviable reputation of being haunted by the shade of the murdered lady.

Travellers forced to pass by after dark held their breath and hurried along on their way, and children were awed into silence in the midst of uproarious mirth by the merest allusion to this fearful dobby–in fact, it had become a positive bugbear to young and old. A few daring spirits would now and then venture on the road, boastingly desirous of seeing the ghost of the poor lady, but their courage always failed them, and they were ready at the least sound, or murmur of the wind, to beat a hasty retreat.

Hence by night

The village matron, round the blazing hearth,
Suspends the infant audience with her tales,
Breathing astonishment! of witching rhymes,
And evil spirits; of the death-bed call
To him who robb'd the widow, and devour'd
The orphan's portion; of unquiet souls
Ris'n from the grave to ease the heavy guilt
Of deeds in life conceal'd ; of shapes that walk
At dead of night, and clank their chains and wave
The torch of hell around the murderer's bed.
At every solemn pause the crowd recoil
Gazing at each other speechless, and congeal'd
With shivering sighs ; till eager for th' event,
Around the beldame all erect they hang,
Each trembling heart with grateful terrors quell'd."

Dr. Akenside's, "Pleasures of Imagination."

CHAPTER III

I____M____ 'was a shrewd, calculating cautious, man, by no means communicative, or desirous of the society of his fellows. There was something not altogether "canny" about him, as the Scotch say, and he was by no means universally beloved.

He enjoyed, more over, an extensive local reputation for curing wounds and some diseases by charms and incantations, mumbling a few strange words and making some peculiar signs over the part affected, so that numbers of persons flocked to him to solicit an exercise of his wonderful gift.

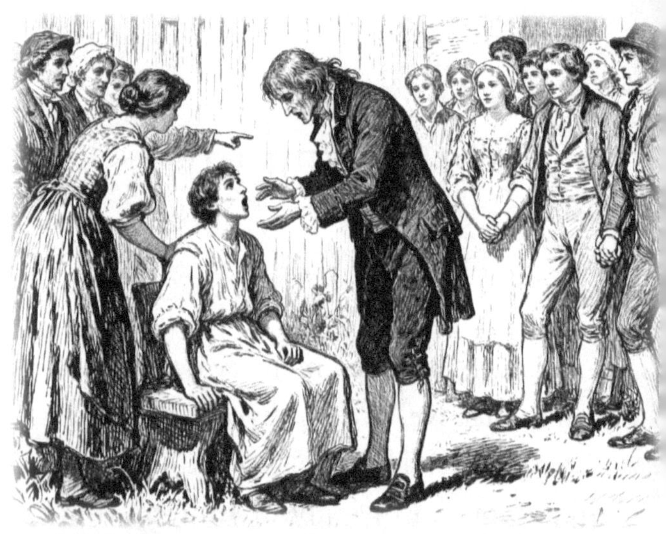

The following charms, at one time used by a man in the neighbourhood of Gloucester, had considerable repute. Each charm was required to be repeated nine times, and the charmer each time to make a movement (in the form of a cross) with his third finger over the part affected : -

"For a canker. O, canker, I do come to tell and to let thee know whereas not to be, and if thou do not soon be gone, some other course I will take with thee."

"For a swell or thorn. Jesus was born in Bethlehem and they crowned him with nails and thorns, which neither blistered nor swelled, so may not this, through our blessed Jesus. Amen."

"For a burn or scald. Mary Miles has burnt her child with a spark of fire. Out fire, in frost, in the name of the Father, Son, and Holy Ghost."-*Brande's Pop. Antiq.*

Altogether he bore a very remarkable character, and became invested with a degree of mystery and awe that had a powerful effect upon the superstitions of that time.

He had not been long at the Old Hall, before the visitations of the "Dobby" became more frequent than formerly, and accompanied by very unpleasant demonstrations.

I____'s face assumed a darker and more forbidding aspect, and people were not slow to remark that the ghost did not approve of his presence in the old house, and that his occupancy as tenant was undoubtedly distasteful to the unfortunate lady's spirit, which sought by these decided manifestations to protest against him for some reason or other.

The farmer thought so himself, and said as much, indeed he felt compelled to wait upon his landlord at the Priory, and inform him that he would be obliged to give up the farm, as his health and that of his family had seriously suffered from the loss of rest, and constant fright of some fearful calamity happening, which had hung over them ever since they had entered on the farm.

He was in a perpetual state of nervous excitement, expecting to see the dreaded apparition every night; that it betokened its near approach by the dismal and unearthly sounds with which they were so unpleasantly familiar, and he concluded with the intimation that he could not remain any longer in the house, or on the farm, where nothing but losses seemed to follow him, unless he were recompensed for his risks, or allowed a substantial reduction in his rent. Even then he did not think he would stay, and he was sure no one else would be found to undertake so very undesirable a situation.

The squire had heard of the bad repute his unfortunate farm had lately fallen into, and how the country people were profoundly impressed with the truth of the stories in circulation.

Rumours had reached him at various times of the strange doings at the Old Hall, how the coming of the spirit was announced by a variety of loud and dreadful noises for a while before its appearance; sometimes rattling in the place like a coach and six, and rumbling up and down the staircase like the trundling of bowls and cannon balls. Then lights had been seen at various times darting about the orchard, and disappearing with sudden rapidity in a flash of pale blue flame.

Once, when the farmer's son lay dying, the door of the invalid's room had been flung open, and the spectre, stalking slowly up to the bed's foot and opening the curtains, looked steadfastly at the sick boy, for a few moments, and then retired as it came.

The landlord was constrained to make allowance for his sorely distressed tenant, and like a kind, liberal gentleman as he was, he very generously offered poor I____ the farm at a mere nominal rent if he would remain and brave the uneasy spirit of his ancestor which seemed "doom'd for a certain term to to walk the night;" but chose most inconveniently the Old Hall Estate as its place of exercise.

It must be recorded that the old squire was not so credulous as it appeared, and although many were shocked at his hardihood, he determined if possible to test most severely the truth of the assertion that the Old Hall was haunted.

He accordingly appointed watchers on different nights, and they were regaled with the best meat and drink, and plenty of tobacco, but they brought him no satisfaction. Not that I____ M____ threw any obstacles in the way–on the contrary, he offered them every facility for their investigations, as he was most desirous the dobby should be "laid."

Sometimes the watchers spent weary vigils with no result, the room they were allowed to occupy exhibiting nothing whatever to cause the slightest uneasiness, until, when they least expected it they would hear the most horrible noises, and sink from their chairs paralysed with fear, nothwithstanding they had previously fortified themselves with plenty of "Dutch courage" to meet the insidious invader of domestic peace. It was very rare that one of those so frighted could be induced to sit up a second time. Besides these precautions, the orchard was carefully examined, anything like a mound was dug up and searched for human bones, a large portion of it was delved to a considerable depth, heaps of stones were removed, and certain suspicious looking fruit trees cut down, in all of which proceedings I_____ assisted with a hearty good will, thereby giving assurance of his intense detestation of the ghostly visitant, and although he was not very talkative upon the subject of his troubles, the continued dejection of his countenance showed how acutely he felt the matter press upon him.

The kitchen floor was torn up and replaced, the ceiling, wainscot, walls, and rafters of the room above were opened out and readjusted, but the mystery remained still unsolved, and the dobby was neither exorcised nor ejected.

CHAPTER IV

" Angels and ministers of grace defend us!
Be thou a spirit of health, or goblin damn'd,
Bring with thee airs from heav'n, or blasts
from hell, Be thy intents wicked or charitable,
Thou com'st in such a questionable shape,
That I will speak to thee."

At length, when volunteers had long since failed to appear, a valiant little man, by profession an attorney's clerk, offered himself as a watch if the squire would provide him with a companion, and accordingly a man of the name of Ritson (sometime butler with the late "parson" Sunderland), was persuaded to come from Bardsea and join in the hazardous adventure by the promise of very liberal remuneration.

The lawyer's name was Goad and he lived on the north side of Soutergate, near the foot of the street. He was remarkable for the rotundity of his person, and the jolly, fearless, good humoured matter-of-fact way in which he met the ups and downs of life, in short, as Mr. Micawber would have said — he was a philosopher.

Mr. Goad and his helper repaired to the Old Hall at the appointed time, and took possession of the room assigned to them by previous arrangement. The same bountiful supply of good things was provided by Colonel Braddyll as had been done on former occasions, but our doughty knight of the quill comported himself discreetly and partook only sparingly of the tempting viands.

At last — about the "wee short hour ayont the twal"— their patience was rewarded, they began to hear noises of the most unaccountable description, and lights flashed across the window of the room in which they were sitting.

Presently the front door opened, and a terrible clanking and lumbering gradually came along the lobby passed upstairs —

crossed the landing — and horror of horrors! approached the apartment they occupied.

The Bardsea man was aghast, but Mr. Goad, who at the first sound had sprung to his feet, and glided stealthily towards the chamber door, waited patiently for the final manifestation of these awful phenomena.

The door was flung violently open — and in an instant the brave little attorney's clerk levelled a blow with his walking stick at the dim outline of a strange figure in the passage — which did not go through it as if it were a mere shadow — but came in contact with a hard material substance, sounding like a human skull, bringing the apparition to the floor with a groan!

*　　*　　*　　*　　*　　*

The other watcher now rushed in, and they both dragged into the candle-light the stunned and bruised corporeal form of M____ the farmer, whose chagrin and disappointment at the discovery of his trick, and the exposure of the long course of deceit he had practised, may be better imagined than described.

He had calculated on the over-strained nerves of the watchers yielding to the influence of the strong waters provided for them, as in the case of many others, and their thus becoming an easy prey to his infernal schemes for terrifying them into unmanly acquiescence in the superstitious tales associated with the Old Hall.

The spectre was habited in an old bonnet and cloak, and had in his hand a heavy iron chain which he had dragged about the passages and stairs in the hope of scaring the bold watchers who were intent upon investigating the alleged nocturnal nuisance.

It afterwards transpired that he had also caused the lights to appear in the orchard by running to and fro with his lantern. Thus was he enabled by his knavery to engraft upon a vague old wife's story an absurb system of spirit-rapping, in order to gain his own selfish and unworthy ends, not even sparing the feelings of his dying boy to establish the notion of a haunted house, but rather expecting the tale to gain additional weight by such undeniable testimony.

It is related that he never forgave those who had detected him in the act of performing his wonted part. Meeting with

Ritson shortly after, he picked a quarrel with him, and challenged him to fight, which being accepted, the battle took place in front of the Hare and Hounds public-house in King Street.

Ritson on that occasion was severely "punished" by the former, and was carried into the inn just named, where he lay ill for a considerable time from the effects of the encounter.

I____ M____ retired subsequently into private life, but his memory is preserved as an instance of the success of unprincipled cunning over educated superstition and ignorant credulity.

The End

www.ingramcontent.com/pod-product-compliance
Lightning Source LLC
Chambersburg PA
CBHW051829180726
48283CB00004BA/1358